Dear Parents:

Congratulations! Your child is taking the first steps on an exciting journey. The destination? Independent reading!

STEP INTO READING® will help your child get there. The program offers five steps to reading success. Each step includes fun stories and colorful art or photographs. In addition to original fiction and books with favorite characters, there are Step into Reading Non-Fiction Readers, Phonics Readers and Boxed Sets, Sticker Readers, and Comic Readers—a complete literacy program with something to interest every child.

Learning to Read, Step by Step!

Ready to Read **Preschool–Kindergarten**
• big type and easy words • rhyme and rhythm • picture clues
For children who know the alphabet and are eager to begin reading.

Reading with Help **Preschool–Grade 1**
• basic vocabulary • short sentences • simple stories
For children who recognize familiar words and sound out new words with help.

Reading on Your Own **Grades 1–3**
• engaging characters • easy-to-follow plots • popular topics
For children who are ready to read on their own.

Reading Paragraphs **Grades 2–3**
• challenging vocabulary • short paragraphs • exciting stories
For newly independent readers who read simple sentences with confidence.

Ready for Chapter
• chapters • longer par
For children who wa
but still like colorful p.

D1114262

books

STEP INTO READING® is designed to give every child a successful reading experience. The grade levels are only guides; children will progress through the steps at their own speed, developing confidence in their reading.

Remember, a lifetime love of reading starts with a single step!

DreamWorks Trolls © 2023 DreamWorks Animation LLC. All Rights Reserved. Published in the United States by Random House Children's Books, a division of Penguin Random House LLC, 1745 Broadway, New York, NY 10019, and in Canada by Penguin Random House Canada Limited, Toronto.

Step into Reading, Random House, and the Random House colophon are registered trademarks of Penguin Random House LLC.

Visit us on the Web!
StepIntoReading.com
rhcbooks.com

Educators and librarians, for a variety of teaching tools, visit us at RHTeachersLibrarians.com

ISBN 978-0-593-43143-6 (trade) — ISBN 978-0-593-48442-5 (lib. bdg.)
ISBN 978-0-593-43144-3 (ebook)

Printed in the United States of America

10 9 8 7 6 5 4 3 2 1

DREAMWORKS

Trolls

Sweet Dance Party!

by Barbara Layman
illustrated by Fabio Laguna and Grace Mills

Random House 🏠 New York

It is spring!
Poppy and Branch
race to Trolls Garden.
Their favorite treats
are ripe and
ready to pick.

"These popberries
are huge," Branch says.

"And yummy!"

says Poppy.

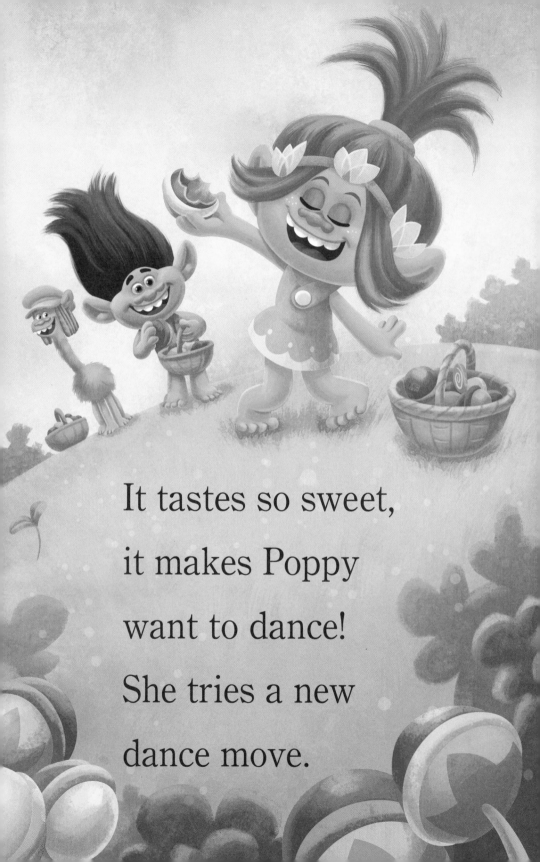

It tastes so sweet,
it makes Poppy
want to dance!
She tries a new
dance move.

Branch tries
a dance move, too.

"Sweet moves, Branch!"
Poppy says.

That gives her an idea!

Poppy makes
fun invitations.
Everyone is invited to her
Sweet Moves Dance Party!

Sheila B. flies
across the skies.
She takes invitations
to all the Trolls.

The invitations say
"Bring your
sweetest moves!"
The Trolls practice
new dances.

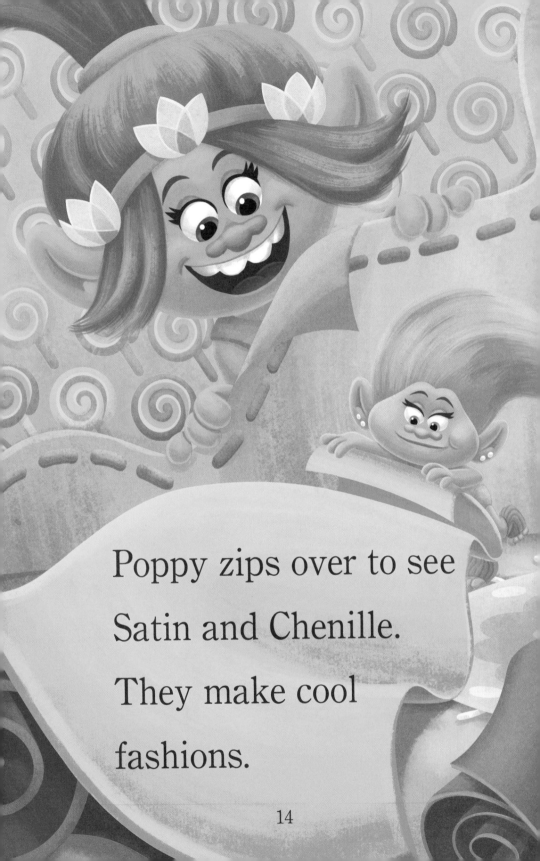

Poppy zips over to see
Satin and Chenille.
They make cool
fashions.

Poppy asks them
to make her
a special dress
for the party.

Later, all the Trolls
arrive at the party.

The music starts.
Prince D and Cooper
show off their
sweet, funky moves.

Guy Diamond shows
his glitter grooves!
Tiny Diamond
dances a
hip-hop bop.

Trollex twists
like a lollipop.
"I call this move
the sweet swirl!"
he says.

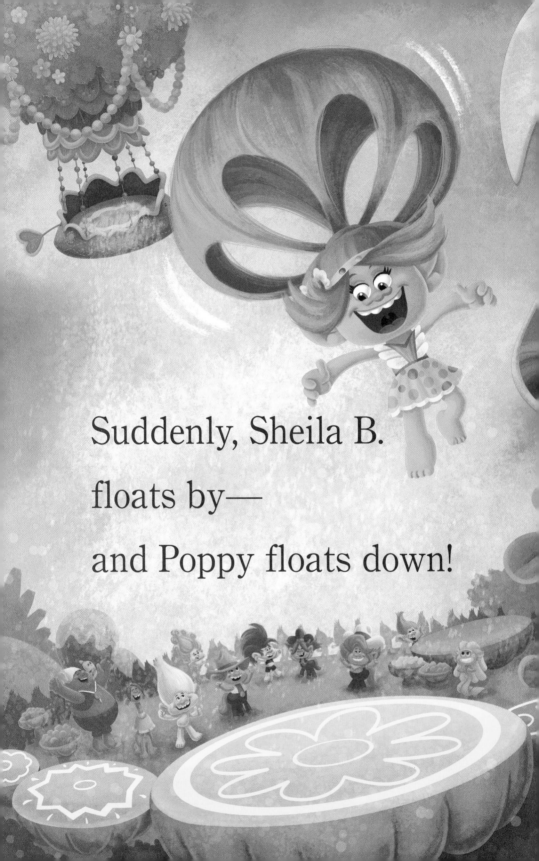

Suddenly, Sheila B.

floats by—

and Poppy floats down!

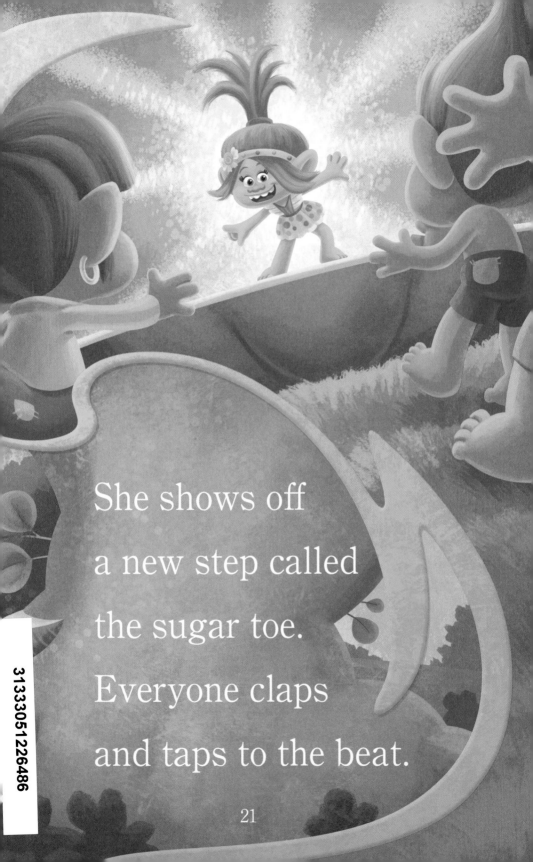

She shows off
a new step called
the sugar toe.
Everyone claps
and taps to the beat.

The Trolls leaders add
their moves to make
one sweet dance.

They call it the
sweet Trolls stroll!

Hooray for

sweet dance moves!